Brewing Love

by

Sara Bourgeois

Blurb

After her latest breakup, Lenora "Lenny" Brewer has had it up to the tippy top with her life in the city. Her job as an online gossip writer isn't what she had planned when she graduated from college with a Journalism degree, and making it to her early thirties without a husband or children wasn't exactly what she'd planned either.

The day after she had to dump her almost-fiancé for emptying out her savings account, Lenny goes into work, and her dreadful boss tells her she's got to write a scathing story about her favorite pop music princess.

Well, that's a step too far. Lenny quits her job, packs her things, and flees the city for her Aunt's bed and breakfast just outside the Shawnee Forest.

When she finds out that the small town where her Aunt lives still has a local paper, and they need an investigative reporter, it's almost too good to be real.

Add in a hunky park ranger, and Lenny starts to think that Tree's Hollow is a wish come true. There's only one thing that could mess up her perfect new home, and that's a touch of magic.

What Lenny doesn't know is that she's a dormant witch, and taking control of her life unlocks powers inside of her that she didn't even know existed.

Oh, and there's the small matter of the murder that occurs shortly after Lenny arrives at the Tree's Hollow Bed and Breakfast. The death of a local curmudgeon has the town on edge, and the county sheriff stumped.

Will she learn to harness the craft brewing inside of her, or will trouble boil over and destroy everything she comes to love?

This book is a cozy mystery with no swearing, violence, or adult content. It is the first book in a new series, and Brewing Love is suitable for all ages.

Dedication

This book is dedicated to the woman who has picked me up every time I have fallen down. I love you, Mom. I'm glad I could make you smile.

One

Hello.

I'm Lenora, "Lenny," Brewer, and my life is a mess. I want to tell you about last night. It was the worst, and it would be funny if it weren't so sad. The man, if you can call him that, which I thought I was going to marry, dropped a pretty big bombshell on me.

It all started when he invited me out to dinner at the fanciest restaurant in the city. We'd been dating for a couple of years and Devon, that's his name, had never taken me there. I was so excited. I thought this was "the" dinner. You know, the one where the guy pops the question over a fancy meal. I figured he was going to wine me, dine me, and then ask me to be his wife with a big diamond ring fit for a princess.

I'm not sure what gave me that idea because Devon has never treated me like a princess, but his choice in the restaurant made me think that maybe he was turning over a new leaf. The fact that he asked me to meet him there for a six-o-clock dinner reservation probably should have tipped me off that things were not going to go as I imagined, but I digress.

The restaurant, The Chef's Table, is pretty busy when I arrive. It's also noisy because, at that hour, the place is full of business people schmoozing clients and celebrating work victories for the day. It's not the most romantic atmosphere, but life is what you make it, right?

Anyway, the restaurant won't seat you until all of your parties arrive, so I had to sit in the waiting area until Devon showed up. He was twenty minutes late, and the hostess threatened to give our table away twice. I ended up slipping her twenty dollars because I didn't want this night to be ruined. It never occurred to me that I was trying and Devon wasn't.

I told myself he was stuck at work or held up in traffic. Perhaps he was at the jewelry store getting my ring, and it was taking longer than he anticipated. It's not as if he'd ever bought an engagement ring before.

Well, that's not true. He'd been engaged once before me, but it had ended badly. His ex-girlfriend kept the ring, and from what he'd said, the breakup had been hard on him.

Okay, so Devon finally shows up, and all he offers me is a "Sorry I'm late babe." and a quick peck on the cheek.

Now, I don't want to complain, but I went home after work and got all dolled up for this dinner. I'm talking little black dress, diamond studs my father gave me for my twenty-first birthday, and black pumps I bought at Saks on the way home. That's right, I didn't even own high heels, but I purchased a pair for this dinner. I put my hair up in a fancy braid ponytail thing I saw on the internet, and I applied just the right amount of makeup. I wanted to look classy, elegant, stylish for the moment Devon asked me to be his forever.

Not only was Devon still wearing his khakis and polo from work, but he didn't compliment me on my dress either. He didn't even really look at me as the hostess was seating us, and he stared at the menu like his life depended on it once we were sitting at our table.

That's when I started to let go of the imaginary evening I had planned for us, and I started paying attention to what was really going on around me. Devon was sweating, red-faced, and super nervous. His clothes were rumpled as if he'd pulled them out of a laundry basket. Clearly, he was not doing so hot.

The waiter came and took our order. Devon ordered the most expensive steak on the menu and a bottle of champagne. I ordered my absolute favorite meal of crab and rosemary pomme fries. Those are basically fancy French fries, but they taste better when you call them that. I've never had them at a place this swanky, though, so I assumed I was in for a treat.

"Hey, sweetie. What's wrong?" I asked and offered him a reassuring smile after the waiter left.

"I need to talk to you about something." He said very quietly.

Oh, here we go. It's not exactly how I thought it would be, but it's happening.

"And, I don't want you to be mad at me." He whispered.

Oh, crud. Maybe Devon just means the ring is smaller than what he wanted. Maybe he's worried about proposing this way. Perhaps he had something even more romantic planned, and it just didn't pan out. Whatever it is, I'm sure it's fine.

"Whatever it is, I'm sure it's fine," I say aloud, and I mean it.

I'm not the kind of woman who is obsessed with a massive diamond engagement ring. It doesn't even have to be a diamond. A sapphire or a ruby would be just as lovely, and I would cherish it.

"I don't know any other way to say this other than to just spit it out. So, that's what I'm going to do." He says a little louder, but not much.

Let's pause for a moment. I want to make sure you understand just how delusional I am at this point. I actually held my hand out for him to slip the ring on my finger. It wasn't nearly as embarrassing as it sounds, though, because Devon didn't even look up from the spot he was staring at on the table.

"I got your pin number out of your desk, and I borrowed your debit card when you were out for a run yesterday." His words hit me like a truck, and I started to feel myself getting queasy. "I went to the ATM on the corner and withdrew most of what was in your savings account."

"What?" I yelled and shot up out of my chair.

If his plan was to bring me to this fancy restaurant and tell me he stole my savings here so that I wouldn't cause a scene, Devon didn't know me at all. That's when it hit me that he didn't know me. Did he really think he could take my life's savings and then just smooth things over with a fancy dinner? A dinner he was late for.

"Please sit down, Lenny. You're making a scene." His lip was quivering, and big, fat crocodile tears were pooling in his eyes.

"You're darn right I'm making a scene. You stole my money. And, don't call me Lenny. My friends and family call me Lenny. You are neither of those things." I hissed.

"Lenny. I mean, Lenora, please calm down. I didn't steal your money, I swear. I just borrowed it. I had an excellent reason."

"You didn't borrow my money. People ask when they borrow money. You stole my debit card and pin number so you could take money out of my account without telling me. I should call the police." At this point, I'm still standing up, and everybody in the restaurant is looking right at me.

"Lenny, please calm down. Please hush." Devon said a little louder.

"I told you not to call me Lenny, and when in the history of the world did telling a woman to calm down ever result in her calming down? And, did you really just tell me to hush?"

"I'm sorry Lenora. My cousin really needed to borrow the money, and I didn't have it. I thought you might be a little upset, but I figured we'd work it out. We can work this out. Please, baby." The crocodile tears started to spill over his cheeks now.

"You stole my life savings to give to your greasy cousin? To what? To pay off some loan shark? Did you really think that was something we could work out?" I sat down when I saw the restaurant manager walking towards our table. I didn't want to, but I also didn't want to get kicked out of this place before I decided if I was going to call the police or just kick his butt.

"I didn't want to take it without asking, but I knew you'd say no." He sniveled.

"That's because I don't want you giving my money to your slimy cousin." I tried to keep my voice down. I really did.

"I didn't give it to him. He's going to pay you back. I swear."

"No, he isn't. You know that as well as I do. I'm never going to see that money again. That was everything I've saved since I graduated from college. I was going to use that money to put a down payment on an apartment." I said and started to take out my phone.

"What are you doing, sweetie?" He said as I started to dial the non-emergency number for the police.

"I'm calling the police. You stole my debit card and emptied out my savings account. What did you think I was going to do?"

Devon started to do that big, ugly cry thing with the snot and body shaking. I almost felt bad for him, except that he stole all of my money. Before I could hit the last number to dial the police, Devon got up and ran out of the restaurant. Just got up out of his chair and bolted.

Leaving me with the bill.

The restaurant was nice enough to box up all of the food I paid for, and a couple of gentlemen offered to run after Devon. I declined their offers even though it was pretty tempting. I needed to get home and call the bank as soon as possible.

I was pleased to find that the restaurant had generously thrown in a crab cracker with my meal, so I wasn't going to have to smash the legs with a hammer I kept in my hall closet. Also, my butter was still warm. I put everything on a plate and put what would have been Devon's meal into my fridge. It wouldn't be as good reheated, but it would still be pretty dang tasty tomorrow for lunch.

Jezebel, my cat, was more than happy to see me since I'd brought crab home. Generally, she ignores me for the most part, but tonight she was at the door waiting for me like a faithful and loving family pet. Jezzy rubbed against my legs and purred as I sat down on the sofa and flipped on the television. She laid her head in my lap, and I almost fell for it.

"You just want some of my meat, don't you?" I said and gave her the skeptical eye.

I swear she winked at me, but that would have been nuts. I'd been single for approximately a half an hour, and I was already turning into a crazy cat lady. That seemed fitting. Here I was thirty-three, single again, no kids, and I worked as a gossip writer on a celebrity website. Most of the people I worked with were ten years, or more, younger than me.

Half of the office called me "grandma" and thought it was funny. I don't remember which little jerk gave me that nickname, but I'm pretty sure he's already been fired. The only reason I'm still working there is that the money is good, and I was saving for an apartment. I wanted a nice place close to the top floor in one of the skyscrapers downtown.

That reminded me that I needed to call the bank. I dialed the number, put the phone on speaker, and set to cracking the crab legs open as quietly as possible in case I got through to a representative in mid-crack.

It must have been a busy night in the customer service department at my bank because, by the time I was off hold, I'd opened all of the crab legs and shared them with Jezebel. Full and happy, she forgot I existed again and wandered off to go take a nap on my pillow.

I talked to Maria, the customer service rep, for ten minutes and my money was back in my account. Apparently, my bank covers me for lost or stolen cards. Maria told me I had to file a police report within seven days, or the bank would take the money back out.

"So, I have to turn him in, or I can't keep my money?" I asked just to be sure.

"Yes, Ma'am. The sooner, the better." Maria answered.

"I can live with that."

I looked at the clock, and it wasn't even eight p.m. yet. It was too early to go to bed, or I'd be up before four. I didn't have any plans, so I decided to head down to the police station and file my report tonight. Maria had given me some numbers and other information to give the police as evidence, so I tucked the paper I'd written it down on into my purse. Once my shoes and jacket were on, I called Uber. A driver showed up in under ten minutes, and I was on my way to the police station.

Looking back, I kind of wish I'd waited until daytime to file the report. Have you even been in a police station at night? It's not exactly what I'd call a wholesome environment. If I'd waited, I'd probably still have my job, and I would have gotten to go on pretending that humanity isn't as bad as I thought.

About the job thing, we'll get back to that later.

For now, the police station was teeming with life. People were crying, cursing, and the man sitting next to me in the waiting area smelled like baby powder and gasoline. His name was Herb, by the way.

Wanda, the front desk officer, looked at me like I was crazy for coming in when I did to fill out a theft report, but she took my information and only made me sit in the waiting area for seven minutes before taking me back to another room. It was exactly seven minutes because I was watching the time go by on my phone.

I filled out the forms she gave me, and Wanda handed them off to a detective. His name was Gary, and he was happy to have someone who hadn't been stabbed to talk to for a few minutes. So, we chatted and drank a Styrofoam cup of bad coffee until he couldn't ignore the people in the waiting room anymore.

"I'll get this over to the District Attorney tomorrow. I'm sure they'll make an arrest. I'll also send the bank the paperwork they need. It's been a pleasure, Lenny." Gary said and shook my hand.

He was smiling when we were done with our conversation, mostly him telling me about his grandkids, but his shoulders slumped a little, and he looked sad as I followed him back out to the waiting area. He ran his hand through his mussed gray hair and called out a name that I didn't entirely listen to.

I just wanted to go home. I got outside and realized I hadn't called Uber yet. The thought of going back inside and waiting for my ride was daunting, but fortunately, for me, a cab pulled up and let a woman and child out. They were both crying, and I wished I could do something to help.

I knew there was nothing I could do, so I needed to get out of there as fast as possible. Getting away from the negative energy emanating from that place felt frantically vital.

Just as I was about to get into the cab and escape, it happened. A black limousine pulled up to the cab, and the back passenger door swung open. Starla Lex stumbled out as if she were pushed and fell onto the sidewalk. I looked at her face, and her cheeks and eyes were all swollen like she had been crying a lot. There was also a nasty bruise on her arm just below the cap sleeve of her red, sequined dress.

"You think I'm such a bad man, why don't you just go in and tell the police all about me!" The voice of her long-term boyfriend Boyd Cotts yelled out from inside the car.

The limo driver was out of the car and around the vehicle in no time. Starla's purse came flying out of the car and landed next to her even as the driver tried to help her up off the pavement.

"Get back in the limo and drive me home!" Boyd yelled at the driver, but the man used his foot to kick the door closed.

He helped Starla get up and walk into the police station, and as I watched in shock, my cab drove away. I took a few steps back from the scene and called Uber. I begged them to hurry and then walked down the block so they wouldn't be picking me up in front this horror show.

I wanted to look away, but I couldn't. As I watched from down the block, two uniformed police officers came out of the station and dragged Boyd out of the limo. They had to cuff him because he wouldn't cooperate, and as I got into my Uber to go home, they were leading him inside.

"Was that Boyd Cotts?" The young woman exclaimed as I clicked my seatbelt in the back of her immaculate Prius.

"I think so," I answered and hoped she would just pull away.

"I'm not sure. I haven't been here long. I came from the other direction." I lied, but I didn't want to talk about it.

"He probably beat up Starla. Everybody knows that guy is a dou..."

"Can we go now? I'm sorry. I'm just so tired." I pleaded with the young, star-struck woman.

"Oh, sure. Sorry."

Two

Okay, so about my job. That's where Starla comes in. You see, Ms. Lex is the pop music world's biggest princess right now. She and Boyd have been the "it" couple for the last three months. Starla has never held onto a man for longer than a couple of weeks since her career began, and the whole world thought that Boyd was her Prince Charming.

That guy is no Prince Charming.

The fact that he's an alcoholic, abusive, jerkwad was starting to come to light slowly. Well, it was slow until last night. Last night was one of those incidences that can make or break a celebrity gossip writer's career, and I had a front row seat.

There is just one problem. I didn't want it. I adore Starla Lex, and it took every ounce of strength I had not to hop into the back of that limo and claw that jerk's eyes out. Especially after what Devon did to me. I was ready to burn my bra and kill all men.

I held myself together and vowed to keep my presence at that scene a complete secret. The last thing I needed was my boss Veronica finding out I was there. She'd want me to write a horrible, juicy story about Starla, and there was no way I was going to do that.

This job made me hate myself enough as it was. Starla was a good girl, and she never got into any kind of trouble. She was an excellent role model for young girls, and that was horrible for my line of work.

Getting the dirt on Starla Lex was the big fish. It could rocket my career as a gossip writer into the stratosphere. Except, I didn't want that. I just wanted to keep my head down and write about awful celebrities, who deserved bad press, until I had enough money for an apartment. Then, I was going to try to get a real job doing real journalism.

The morning after the break-up, which I was surprisingly not that sad about, and the police station incident I got up and got ready for work just like any other day.

Jezebel was sitting on my chest promptly at five thirty a.m. with her paws on my collarbone. She yowled and dug her claws in just a bit when I didn't move fast enough.

"Yes, yes. Breakfast for the queen." I said and scratched under her chin.

She hopped down and sashayed into the kitchen, so I could fill her food bowl with the grain-free, soy-free, no preservatives or additives cat food that she insisted on eating. Queen indeed. I understand, though. I like good food too.

Next, it was shower and then pick out the perfect outfit that doesn't make me look too old but also doesn't make it look like I'm trying too hard to look younger. Then it's make-up and hair.

After I'm done trying way too hard to look like I'm not trying at all, I finally get to sit down to my breakfast. I learned a while ago that I'm a very cranky person if I don't get a good, hot breakfast into myself before work. I don't have time to cook every morning, so I cook a batch something tasty on the weekends to heat up on work days.

This week it's breakfast burritos. Scrambled eggs, Chihuahua cheese, chorizo, peppers, roasted potatoes, and very thinly sliced sautéed onion all wrapped up in an artisanal whole wheat and corn tortilla. I heat it up and sit down at my tiny kitchen table. I like to eat my breakfast and stare out the window at all of the people scrambling back and forth on their way to whatever the day holds.

Jezebel stares at me for a few minutes like she can't believe I'm not sharing, so I hold the burrito down and let her have a sniff. She hisses at the burrito and runs out of the room. I assume she's going to go lie down on my pillow and have a nap now that her belly is full.

I have a confession to make. I know it sounds like I'm some big fancy city girl, but the website I work for doesn't even have offices in the city. I live in one suburb, and my office is in another. I take the commuter train to work every day, so the station is where I go once I'm finished with breakfast.

Since it takes a while to get there, I always bring a book. I get through one or two a week, just on my train rides to and from work.

Once I'm there, I grab a coffee from the guy who runs the coffee cart in the lobby, and I head upstairs to my cubicle. Typically, I start scanning social media, aggregation sites, and discussion boards for leads, but today that's not going to happen.

When I walk into the bullpen, everyone is staring at me. I don't know why I thought I could keep it a secret that I was there when Starla got kicked out of her own limo last night, but someone had been recording it on the phone. I was in the video watching the whole thing go down.

A hush fell over the office when Veronica opened her door. "I need to see you, Lenny. Now." She said and slammed the door.

Everybody scrambled and tried to pretend like they'd been busy little worker bees all along. "Thanks for the support guys," I mumbled under my breath as I made my way across the floor to Veronica's office.

When I got inside, the real fun began.

"Close the door, Lenny." She said and took a sip of her hot chai.

Veronica peered up at me over the tops of her very trendy black glasses. She didn't even need glasses but insisted they gave her the air of a real journalist. I'm 100% confident that Veronica doesn't know the definition of journalism.

"How can I help you, Veronica?" I say hoping that if I play dumb, this will somehow all go away.

Maybe she'll forget why she called me in here. Perhaps she'll remember what a big fan of Starla Lex I am and not make me write the piece she's about to ask me to write. Maybe a meteor will hit the building.

"I saw the video of you last night with Starla Lex. I know you didn't call me right away because you've been working on a secret article you'll have on my desk at three p.m. Right, Lenny?" She turned her chair and started typing away at her keyboard.

The implication was that there was nothing else to say. I was to do the article whether I liked it or not, and it better be good.

"Veronica, I think that we should honor Starla's privacy on this. What I saw last night wasn't something the world needs to know about. It's a very painful thing she's going through." I almost sounded like I was pleading.

"Well, it's a good thing we don't pay you to protect celebrities privacy." She said, and it stung. "Now, I don't want the version of the story I saw on the video. I want the special Lenny Brewer version of the story. The one no one else has. The one where beautiful and perfect Starla Lex got in a drunken brawl with her boyfriend and got dragged into the police station seconds before he got dragged in too. Now, go out to your desk and give me what I want, or take a hike. You're a hack, and there are plenty more hacks waiting in line for this job. I could find someone younger and hungrier than you like that." Veronica said and snapped her fingers.

I jumped at the sound, and in a state of shock walked back out to my desk. As I booted up my computer, a strange feeling started to take over me. It was like nothing I'd ever experienced before in my life.

I was done.

It was as if I'd run out of excuses. I was always trying to make excuses for people and be the reasonable one when they treated others and I like a doormat. However, all of a sudden, I was out. I just couldn't do it anymore. I couldn't make one more excuse for the way Veronica was treating me. Normally I would have told myself that she just wanted the website to be successful and that she believed in me so much that she knew she could be tough.

That was complete bull honkey.

Veronica was a self-absorbed nitwit who made money off of other people's suffering, and I had been an accomplice all these years. It was time for me to participate in my second ugly scene in twenty-four hours.

First I needed to pack up my desk so that I could make a grand exit after I told Veronica off. I didn't want to have to come back out here and box up my stuff while security watched me.

I threw my picture of Devon in the trash and gave the frame to Claudia. She sat three cubes down from me and really liked it, so I figured I'd give her a parting gift. The rest of my stuff fit in a box I found in the basement. My laptop, knick-knacks from my ledge, and a picture of Jezebel all fit neatly in the box. Once it was packed, I marched into Veronica's office.

"I quit, Veronica. There is nothing I want in this world enough to make me spend one more day in this place or one more ounce of my integrity on this publication." I set the box down on her desk so I could put air quotes around "publication."

I didn't wait for her to respond. Instead, I picked up my box and headed for the elevator. I'd like to say that people clapped and cheered for me as I made my way out of our office, but most of them just stared at me in wide-eyed horror. The rest of them scurried away as if whatever I'd just done was contagious.

Veronica poked her head out of her office as the elevator doors were closing."You can't quit because you're fired."

"Whatever, Veronica," I said and flipped her the bird.

I felt pretty triumphant at that moment, although I'm pretty sure the doors were already closed by the time I flipped her off. It still totally counts.

As I rode the train home, I tried not to think about what would happen if the bank took the money back out of my account. I had my savings back for now, but what if the bank decided he didn't steal it? What if they thought I was in on it? What if I quit my job, lost all of my savings, and I went to jail?

I was sure that Devon would tell them he didn't steal the money and that I'd said he could have it. All of a sudden, I couldn't breathe. The walls of the train started to close in on me as I pictured the police leading me off in handcuffs. I thought of Jezebel at home all alone starving for two days while I waited for someone to get me out of the pokey, and black spots started to swim in front of my eyes as I hyperventilated.

Right before I passed out, a nice man in the seat next to me put his hand on my shoulder reassuringly and asked me if I was okay. Only, he startled me so badly that I screamed.

That's when the train stopped, and the lights went out. Not in my head either. Like, literally the train stopped, and the power went out. The elderly man next to me, who looked a little shaken by my screaming in his face, took my hand and told me to breathe.

So, I did. He coached me through several long deep breaths until I was calm again. Thankfully, about the time I got ahold of myself, the lights came back on, and the train started moving again.

Things got a little bit hazy after that. I remember thanking the man as I got off at my stop. At least, I hope that's a real memory. Jezebel looked a little puzzled when I came through the door so early, but she didn't complain because I fed her again. I always fed her when I got home, and it slipped my mind that I was about seven hours earlier than normal.

I started to snap out of my haze a little bit, so I decided to take a long, hot bath and start this day over again. As I soaked in hot water and watched the bubble float towards the ceiling, I made a decision.

"It's time for a significant change," I said to Jezebel who was sitting on the bathroom counter watching my every move.

Three

As soon as I'd gotten out of the tub, I started putting my plan into action. Since I didn't have to go back to work, I pulled on my most comfortable pair of black yoga pants and a slouchy gray sweatshirt. I took my laptop out of the box from work and booted it up. Much to my delight, there was a place that rented moving vans just a few blocks away from my house. Instead of making the booking online, I actually picked up the phone and called them.

"Well, Ma'am if you'd called fifteen minutes ago, you'd have been out of luck. But, someone just dropped one off. Give me about thirty minutes to clean it and process it back into my inventory and it's all yours."

Thirty minutes gave me enough time to walk to the rental place, so I decided to do that instead of calling Uber. Before I slipped on my black Doc Martins, I called my one and only friend, Joy.

You see, when you're in the business of trashing celebrities on the internet, it's hard to form trusting relationships. Pair that with the fact that I'm kind of a loner, and you get a lady with a cat and one friend. I had a boyfriend, but ya'll already know how that went.

"Come over and help me pack," I said when Joy picked up the phone.

"Pack for what?" She sounded about as unthrilled with the idea as a person could possibly be.

"I'm moving. I want to leave today. Come help me pack up my place and say goodbye. I'll buy you lunch and dinner. Oh, and all the snacks you want too."

"Lenny, I'm at work," Joy said, and I could almost hear her rolling her eyes.

"Yeah, so? You've taken zero of your vacation or paid time off days in the last five years. When was the last time you even called in sick? Just leave for the day. I'm sure the world will happily wait for your services." I was practically pleading because I wanted to leave, but I didn't want to skip town without telling Joy goodbye in person.

Joy and I are both extreme introverts. We live in the same suburb, and we've still done most of our recent "hanging out" over Skype. We call it being alone together.

Joy doesn't have many friends either, but that's because she does audits for the IRS. She really loves her job, which is why she never takes time off, and that disturbs people. I like her. She's got a dry sense of humor that really cuts to the quick. When she actually makes jokes that is.

"Fine. I'll make up the time before the next pay period. I don't mind coming in early and staying late for the next six work days. Especially since I get to spend time with you packing things into boxes." She was teasing.

"Whatever floats your boat. I'm going to walk over and pick up the moving van. I'll see you at my place in an hour." I say with an excitement Joy does not share.

She grumbles something about me needing a lobotomy and agrees to meet me. Then I figure that I should at least call my Aunt Kara and confirm that she does have room for me at her bed and breakfast.

"Aunt Kara? Hi, it's Lenny. I was calling about a room at your place."

"It's already reserved for you, Sweetie. I'm going to be so glad to see you." She said, and the sound of her voice washed away any doubt I was having about this move.

"Wait? What did you mean it's already reserved?"

"You'll understand more when you get here. You guys have fun packing, and make sure you drive safe." Aunt Kara said with a smile on her face that I could hear in her voice.

"Thanks, Aunt Kara. I love you."

"Love you too, Brat."

I'd almost forgotten that she used to call me Brat. It was a joke because when I was a kid, I'd been the polar opposite of a brat. I was quiet, studious, and well mannered, and Aunt Kara found it utterly bizarre.

She believed that children were meant to be rambunctious and rude, and Kara tried at every turn to get me into some kind of trouble. It probably wasn't the most responsible thing for her to do, but we sure did have a lot of fun.

I slipped a pair of gloves on and wrapped a scarf around my neck. It wasn't chilly enough for a coat, but I knew that after I'd walked a couple of blocks, my hands would get cold. I walked quickly towards the truck rental place. It felt like a new chapter in my life was opening up before me, and I was in a hurry to turn the next page.

The man I spoke to on the phone had the van and the paperwork ready by the time I got to the store. There wasn't a drop off location in Tree's Hollow, but there was a location an hour away. I'd figure that part out when I got there.

I took the van and parked it in the underground parking space provided by my apartment building. Thankfully, I had a spot and no car parked in it, so I didn't have to worry about what to do with the van while I packed up everything in my home.

When I got back upstairs, I made café and cocoa for Joy and me. It's a mixture of coffee and hot cocoa, and it's Joy's favorite hot drink. My doorbell rang just as I poured the hot drink into the mugs, and I buzzed her in.

Joy came in, and we sat at my kitchen table for the last time drinking our café and cocoa in complete silence. I would miss having someone to sit around and do nothing with, but I knew that new adventures awaited me in Tree's Hollow.

Once our drinks were gone, Joy and I got busy packing. She'd brought a huge pile of boxes from home, and there were even more outside the basement storage in my building.

It was relatively easy to pack up my entire apartment. Since I'd been saving for a new place, I hadn't bought much for myself over the years. Most of my books and collectibles from when I was a kid were in storage near Aunt Kara's bed and breakfast. I still read a ton, but most of my books were eBooks now, and they didn't require packing.

After a few hours of boxing, taping, and traipsing up and down the stairs, we had everything but the furniture. It only took us a couple of hours to disassemble my furnishings and carry them downstairs too.

"Thanks for the café and cocoa. I'll come see you soon." Joy said and gave me a quick hug.

"Wait, that's it?" I said, but I was surprised she'd hugged me.

"Like you said, I've got about three years of vacation time saved up. Get settled and give me a call. I like the forest, it's quiet, and there aren't a lot of people." She said and then left.

I took a quick look around my empty apartment and felt Jezebel rub against my legs. She purred, and I got the feeling Jez was as excited about the move as I was. Everything was lining up perfectly, and it was as if the universe was moving obstacles out of my way.

"You've got to get in the crate," I said and opened the door on the cat carrier.

"Meow."

"You've got to get in the crate, Jezebel. At least until we get out of the city. Please." I pleaded with my sassy cat.

"No."

"Please, Jezebel. I'll let you ride in the seat after we're on the road. I promise." I promised. "Wait, did you just say No? or Meow?"

"Meow."

"I'm losing my mind. I could swear you just told me no. If you did, please do it again."

"Meow," Jezebel said and reluctantly walked into the carrier.

I made good on my promise and let Jezebel out of the crate as soon as we passed the city limits. She sat on the seat with her paws on the van's window ledge and watched the scenery roll by. I could swear she was as excited as I was, but it was hard to tell because she's a cat.

When I was about half way to Southern Illinois, I could hear my stomach rumbling. I pulled off the road onto the parking lot of a diner. The thought of leaving Jezebel locked in the van wasn't appealing, so I looked up the restaurant's number on my phone and called in a take-out order.

There wasn't much to do, so Jez and I sat in the van and watched videos on my phone for the fifteen minutes the diner said it would take for my order to be ready. She curled up on my lap and fell asleep just in time for me to have to get up.

"I'm sorry, girl," I said as I laid her down on the passenger seat. "I'll be right back."

She lifted up her head for a second but then fell back to sleep. When cats sleep, they really commit to it. I locked her in the van and went inside. It was after regular dinner hours, so the diner was dead. I paid cash and was in and out in a few minutes.

I wanted to get back on the road, but if I wrecked the van because I was eating and driving, I'd never forgive myself. It only took me ten minutes to eat my fish and chips. That's with having to pick pieces of the white fish out of the batter and feed them to Jezebel. I thought she was thoroughly exhausted, but apparently, she had enough energy to beg for food.

Driving after dark was a less than perfect idea. No one got hurt, but I started to wonder if I'd drifted off to sleep or something during part of the drive. It's all a little unclear, but for some reason, the drive took a lot less time that I expected.

After I pulled out of the diner, the rest of the trip to Tree's Hallow should have taken a few hours, but it felt like it took under an hour. When I arrived at Tree's Hollow Bed and Breakfast I looked at the clock on the dash of the van, but it had gone out.

Jezebel woke up and stretched her legs, and I forgot about the time. I grabbed my suitcase and her, and together the two of us went into the giant Victorian mansion.

Walking in took my breath away. I hadn't visited my Aunt in years, but I had so many childhood memories of this place. It hadn't changed a bit. The burgundy brocade wallpaper hadn't aged a day, and the lights on the walls still looked like gas lamps. The lobby was quiet, and Lenny's boots barely made a sound on the dark wood floors.

Jezebel wriggled violently and worked her way out of my grip. Her paws hit the floor with a soft thud, and she ran up the stairs ascending from the lobby before I could react.

"Jezebel," I whispered because I didn't want to attract the attention of the man behind the desk.

"It's fine. I'm sure she knows where she's going." The man behind the counter said as he looked at me over the book he was reading.

"Excuse me?"

"Jezebel. I'm sure she knows what room to go to, Lenny." He responded.

"You know my name?"

"It hasn't been that long, has it?" He asked and raised his eyebrows at me. "It's me, Nick Strunk. I've worked for your Aunt since you were little."

"Oh my gosh, Nick. You look great."

And, it was true. Nick had to be in his fifties by now, but he didn't look like he'd aged since I was a little girl. He'd been in love with Aunt Kara since they were in elementary school together. Nick had helped her open the place. Aunt Kara had never given in and agreed to go on a date with him, but he wouldn't give up. She gave him a job in the

B&B working the desk at night figuring he'd give up eventually and move on. He never did.

"Thanks. I've got your room all ready for you."

I walked over to the desk and sat my suitcase down. Nick handed the key across the counter to me, and I looked over the tree-shaped keychain attached to it.

"Don't most places have those electronic key thingies now?" I asked.

"Yep, but since when has Your Aunt ever done what other people do?"

"You're right," I had said before a big yawn escaped from me. "Ugh. I'm more tired than I thought."

"Get up to bed then. I'll see you tomorrow night."

I picked up my luggage and started up the stairs. I ran my hand up the polished wooden balustrade the way I did every time I went up these stairs as a kid. When I reached the second floor, I turned to the left instinctively and saw Jezebel lying in front of the door at the end of the hall.

As soon as she saw me, she rolled onto her back and started to swish her tail against the thick cream carpeting. I made my way down the hall and used the key to open the door. Jezebel was impatient, and she pushed her way past me into the room as soon as I cracked the door.

When I got into my room, the frantic pace of the day hit me. I couldn't tell what time it was because the clock next to the bed was suffering from the same malfunction as the one in the van, but I knew I was tired.

I opened my suitcase and pulled out my fuzzy sheep pajama pants. After I was dressed and ready for bed, I slipped under the covers. I fell asleep almost instantly. The last thing I remembered before drifting off was Jezebel jumping onto the bed and curling up beside me.

I had the strangest sensation of falling as unconsciousness took me, but it wasn't frightening. It was as if a balance was being set inside of me. I was falling into myself, and then I was gone.

Four

I awoke to the scent of fresh cinnamon rolls and bacon. I sat straight up in bed and scared the bejeezus out of Jezebel. The smell was overwhelmingly divine, and I actually had to wipe a bit of drool from the corner of my mouth.

"That smells fantastic. Oh, sorry Jez. I didn't mean to frighten you."

I jumped out of bed and made my way for the room door. I have no idea why, but absolutely could not resist the smell of those cinnamon rolls. It was almost like magic.

"I'm going downstairs to grab some breakfast. Can I get you anything?" I had asked Jezebel before I went out the door.

"Just a carton of milk, please."

"Okay, see you in a few. Don't destroy the room."

I went downstairs and followed the scent into the breakfast room. Aunt Kara was there dressed in an apricot apron and a 1950's style dress. It was both completely charming and absolutely hilarious. She looked beautiful, but the look didn't fit her personality at all.

"Brat!" She called out and crossed the room quickly to embrace me.

Her hair smelled of honeysuckle. It immediately took me back to the time I was balancing on the fence outside the inn, and I fell off. I skinned me knee so badly that I thought I was going to die.

Aunt Kara rocked me in her arms until my sobs subsided. She was also the only person I would let re-bandage my knee until it was healed. I cried, sobbed, and carried on, but it meant more to me than she'll ever know. I wasn't always the best patient, but the times she cared for me are the times in my life that I felt the most loved.

"Aunt Kara. It's so good to see you. It's been to long." I said and then I was crying in her arms again.

"Let it out, Brat. Let it all go."

Just like that, I felt better. My tears dried up, and the smile returned my face. The scent of breakfast filled my nose again, and I actually felt my new life begin.

Aunt Kara grabbed us two cinnamon rolls, a big pile of bacon, and two coffees. She even brought a packet of hot cocoa for me to mix into my coffee. I wasn't sure how she knew I'd want it, but she knew. It was as if she'd been waiting for this day.

"This is all surreal, Aunt Kara. My life has changed so much in the last two days. I had no idea any of this was coming." I said and took a bite of the cinnamon roll.

The warm, sweet frosting melted in my mouth, and my apprehension vanished with it. I felt my shoulders relax and my breathing deepen as I chewed the perfect texture of the pastry.

"Feel better?" She asked and smiled.

"I do."

"Good, then we'll tackle the small issue of your talking cat."

"What?" I dropped my fork, and it bounced off the plate and onto the floor.

"Keep it down. Finish your cinnamon roll, and we'll talk as soon as breakfast is over." She said and took another bite of her food.

That was the moment that Jezebel asking for milk as I left the room came rushing back to me. Aunt Kara's sweet smile was the same one she used to plaster across her face every time she had to take me to the doctor for shots. Something was about to go down.

Kara finished her roll quickly and excused herself from the table. She had to finish hostessing breakfast before we could talk. Every time I would start to get tense about the things that were going on around me, I would take another bite of the breakfast Kara gave me, and I'd relax again. Even the bacon was the perfect combination of salty, savory, crispy goodness. The food almost felt magical.

Once the last guest left the breakfast room, a young woman in a French maid's uniform came out of a door on the other side of the room. Aunt Kara removed her apron and handed it to the woman who took it back into the room she came from. As Aunt Kara took her seat at the table with me, the woman reappeared and started to clean up.

"Go ahead and ask," Kara said as she crossed her legs and adjusted the hem of her dress.

"Why is your housekeeper wearing a French maid's uniform?" I'm pretty sure that's not the question she was expecting, but I had to know.

"Oh. Okay. That's Evette. She just likes that uniform. I provided her slacks and a black button-down shirt. I figured it would be more comfortable, but Evette bought that dress."

"Evette eh. Is she French? That name sounds French."

"She's not French. Evette just has a very clear idea of who she is and what she likes." Kara said.

"I envy her that," I said.

"I'm confident you're a great deal more like her now than you were two days ago."

"I've changed the subject again. I'm not sure why, but in the last twenty minutes, the fact that my cat is now talking no longer seems strange. I do have to take her some milk soon." I said and took the last swig of my coffee.

"You should. She's not going to like being made to wait too long. Then you have a job interview at nine. The editor in chief of the Tree's Hollow Tribune is looking forward to meeting with you." She said and stood up.

"Wait, I have a job interview? For what job?" I couldn't believe that I already had a job interview.

"Charles will explain everything dear? Now, I have a conference call with some Japanese diplomats that want to stay here after they visit Springfield." Find me later, and we'll have some dinner together. "Oh, and Evette." She turned and called for the housekeeper. "Evette, would you be a dear and grab Lenny a carton of fresh cream for her cat."

Evette hurried into the back room and reappeared with a small container of heavy cream. She put it on the table and flashed a million-dollar smile at me.

"Your kitty will like this much better than plain old milk. We keep a stash in the kitchen for the guests that request it. Most people are happy with milk or half-n-half, but some people only want cream." She said.

"Thank you."

"You're welcome. I'm here until four. Just let the front desk know if you need me for anything."

She went back to her cleaning, and I realized that I needed to get a move on if I was going to get to my interview on time. I took the cream upstairs and poured some of it into one of the glasses from the bathroom.

"Thank you," Jezebel said and licked her paw lazily before diving into the cream.

"I suppose I'm just expected to accept that you're a talking cat now," I said as I walked back into the bathroom to start the shower.

"Ooh, this is cream. And yes, you're going to have to get used to me talking. I have a lot to say, lady." Jezebel said and went back to greedily lapping up the cream.

"Oh really? Like what?" I was going to regret asking, and I knew it.

"You fart in your sleep." She said without looking up at me.

"What?" My cheeks turned bright red.

"You pass gas when you're dreaming."

"Jezebel!"

"I don't mind. I just thought you might like to know." She said, and I could swear she was smiling impishly.

"I don't believe you." I crossed my arms.

I guess I figured that if I got angry, I could stop being embarrassed. Jezebel continued drinking her breakfast while I glowered at her.

"Fine. I made that up, but you do snore like a chainsaw when you have a cold." Jezebel said and went back to licking her paw.

"I can live with that. More cream?"

"Thank you."

After that, I took my shower and got dressed. Jezebel sat right on my feet while I curled my hair and put on a touch of mascara.

"I thought you were some sort of enlightened being. Why are you getting fur all over my pants and shoes?" I asked while looking down at her.

"Still a cat, Lady." She said and then ran off to climb the curtains in protest.

"I have to go. I'll be back soon. Please don't destroy the place while I'm gone." I pleaded.

"Leave the door open, so I can explore." She said still clinging to the thick velvet curtains.

"I can't do that. You can't just run around here." I said, and she jumped down.

"Fine, I'll just poop in here, and I'll shred every piece of fabric in this room. You'll be so mad that you'll put me up for adoption, and maybe my next family will appreciate the fact that I'm a freaking talking cat. Jeeze, Lady." She said and flexed one of her claws at me.

"Okay, okay. I'll leave the door open. Just please promise me you'll behave." I begged. "And stop calling me *Lady*. We've been friends for years."

"Whatever, Lady. Good luck at your interview."

I huffed, scratched her under the chin, and then left the room. The door stayed open. Aunt Kara was in the lobby as I was leaving, so I let her know about Jezebel's newfound freedom. She told me not to worry. Apparently, the inn has a greenhouse in the back yard, and Aunt Kara grows catnip. She figured Jezebel would spend most of the day out there.

Aunt Kara also gave me the keys to her car. She said one of the bell hops would unload my moving van today and put my things in my room and in storage. They'd also return the van for me.

"You don't have to do this," I said.

"Get going, or you'll be late. I've already put the address to the paper into the GPS for you."

So with that, I was on my way to the Tree's Hollow Tribune for my job interview. The funny part was, I didn't really know what job I'd be interviewing for today.

I'd been in the city too long, and the drive to the newspaper was awe inspiring. From my vantage point, the trees seemed taller than the buildings in the city. I knew it was an illusion, but it was almost magical. The trees had the smallest smattering of baby leaves and buds and the brown color with tiny bursts of green and red against the clear blue sky was enchanting.

The GPS told me to turn, so I slowed down and took a right onto a narrow, but paved road. I drove for another mile or so amongst the majestic trees and arrived at what appeared to be a large log cabin.

The Tribune's sign was also made of a large plank of dark wood stained a deep red-brown. The place instantly felt like home in a way that my cubicle at my former job never did.

"Hello, Ms. Brewer! Come in. Would you like some tea?" The older gentleman seated behind his desk called out to me as I walked inside.

"Yes, that'd be great." It had been years since I drank tea, but I figured I'd give it a shot. "I'm afraid you have me at a disadvantage, though. You know my last name, and I only know your first."

"Indeed. I'm Charles Zapier." He said as he walked towards me with his hand extended. "Editor-in-Chief of the Tree's Hollow Tribune."

"It's a pleasure to meet you, Mr. Zapier. Thank you for seeing me today." I said as I took his hand.

"The pleasure is all mine, Lenny. May I call you Lenny? And please, call me Chuck now that the formalities are out of the way." He said and started to walk towards a doorway on the inside wall of the office.

"You can call me Lenny, Chuck. Should I sit down?"

"Please follow me. We'll have our tea in the sitting room. The office is much too formal a place for our chat." He said, and I followed him into a room furnished with two leather couches positioned around a glass and oak coffee table.

In the middle of the room was a huge roaring fireplace like you'd see in a grand hunting lodge. On the other side of the fireplace was a kitchen. The teapot on the stove was already starting to whistle.

I sat down on the sofa facing the window and waited for Chuck to return with the tea. As I waited, I ran my hands nervously over the leather I was seated on, and I noted that it was as soft as butter.

"I wasn't sure how you liked your tea, so I brought everything."

Chuck placed a silver tray on the table. In addition to the teapot, it held two cups, lemons, a sugar dish, honey, and a container of cherries.

"Honestly, I'm not sure how I like my tea either. I'll just try mine the way you drink yours and go from there."

"Sounds like a plan." He said and poured tea into the cups.

After Chuck had dropped two cherries, a thin slice of lemon, and a huge dollop of honey into the cups, he handed me mine and took a seat. We exchanged pleasantries for a few minutes, but eventually it was time to get down to business.

"So, Lenny, I'm not sure how much your Aunt told you about the position, but what I need is an investigative reporter. Is that something that you'd be interested in?" Chuck asked and took a sip of his tea.

This had to be too good to be true. Of course, I wanted the job that Chuck was offering me, but it just seemed so strange.

"I'm very interested, but I need to ask you a question. Why do you need an investigative reporter in Tree's Hollow?" I also wanted to ask him why he needed one now, but I didn't want to push my luck.

"Ah, that's a good question. I see I've made the right decision when it comes to you. " He said and stroked his chin thoughtfully. "Now, as to why I need an investigative reporter, and why I need one now. That's simple." I'm pretty sure he just read my mind. "Print media is pretty much dead, but around here, we've got a lot of folks that like the old ways. They like their morning paper with a cup of coffee, and they don't want to read it on a screen. So, they're willing to pay real money for the product I produce. Oh, and Tree's Hollow isn't the only town around here that likes their newspaper made out of actual paper. We serve several small towns in many local counties. I sell a couple thousand papers a day, and at a dollar twenty-five per paper, I'm sure you can see where the math leads. It only costs me twenty-five cents to produce the papers too."

"I see," I say and try to keep my best poker face.

"I can offer you this as a starting salary." Chuck writes something down on a piece of paper and slides it across the table to me. "Now, if you can produce compelling stories that justify me raising the price of the Tribune to say two dollars, I would split the extra profits with you."

I looked at the paper, and the number was twice what I was making in the city. If you paired that with the lower cost of living here, I would be beyond set financially.

Five

Of course, I couldn't turn the offer down. I was going to be paid to explore my new environment, and I would finally get paid to write real stories.

There were three desks in the Tribune's office. One of them was Chuck's, but I had to choose between the other two. Fortunately, one of the empty desks looked out a huge bay window on the side of the office area. Naturally, I chose that one.

"Who is supposed to sit at the other desk?" I asked as I spun in my new office chair.

"We had a columnist at one point. She retired a few years ago. I've been writing the columns. Hey, that's a splendid idea." Chuck said, and I wasn't sure what he meant because I hadn't given him any ideas. "We should split the columns. I could throw a few hundred more dollars a month your way."

"Sure. What columns are there?"

"Let's see. I've been doing auto repair, cleaning tips, advice, and there's one on the local paranormal phenomenon. They're all written in columns where I answer letters. I do get some of them as emails, but mostly they still come in snail mail."

"Please don't tell me you want me to take cleaning tips and the advice column," I said and rolled my eyes.

"I'll have you know I rather enjoy the cleaning tips column. Do you know anything about auto repair?" He said and raised an eyebrow.

"No," I admitted sheepishly.

"Then it's settled. You take the advice column and the paranormal stuff. That one's real fun. It's not so much questions as it is a collection of sightings and such." He said and picked up a box of letters off the floor.

"Welcome to the team Mrs. Constance Piper and Mr. David Fox." He said and retrieved the second box of letters from the floor next to his desk.

"Those are the names of the columnists?"

"Tilly, the woman whose place you're taking, came up with Constance's name. I came up with the Fox name for the paranormal column." He said with a proud smile.

"You totally ripped that off from that TV show." I teased.

"Do you want the money or not?"

"Yes, sir. Constance David Piper Fox at your service."

Chuck disappeared through another door that I figured out led to a staircase because a few moments later, I could hear him moving around above me. He came back down the stairs and handed me a laptop. It was new in the box, and it looked expensive.

"I have a laptop," I said, but I was drooling over the fancy computer he'd just handed me.

"Is it as nice as that one?"

"No," I responded and turned the box over in my hands.

"Exactly."

The rest of the morning, we sat quietly in the office. The only sound was the clacking of Chuck's keyboard. I read through old columns to get a feel for how they were written, and I tried to brainstorm ideas for my first investigative article. Around noon, the keyboard clicking stopped suddenly.

"Lunch time is going home time. Have a good afternoon. Email me if you start working on a story today. Otherwise, I'll see you tomorrow morning."

"That's it? We go home now?" I asked.

I was so used to being stuck in my cubicle for eight hours or more each day. The thought of being able to leave at lunch time almost made me giddy.

"You can stay here if you want. I've left a key to the office in your desk drawer. The offices are quite nice, but you can go too. At some point, I imagine you'll need to be out in the field. Oh, and you've got your laptop. If you want to write, you can do that anywhere." He said and grabbed his hat and jacket.

I packed up the new laptop, put the box of old columns in Kara's car, and headed back to the inn. I figured if I got tired of being in my room, Aunt Kara might let me spread out in the breakfast room since it wouldn't be used again until tomorrow morning.

I was not expecting the scene I encountered as I pulled into the bed and breakfast's parking area. A crowd was standing outside on the front lawn. Some of the people were congregated together in a large group, and there were smaller groups splintered off around the edge of the bigger mass as well.

One police cruiser with its berries and cherries lit up was parked outside the front door. I read the door on the car.

County Sheriff

I parked my car as far out in the small lot as I could and got out. For a minute, I wasn't sure what to do so I just stood there next to Kara's car.

"This can't be good," I said to myself.

"Dead guy in the parlor," Jezebel said.

I didn't even see her approach me, but there she was sitting on the hood of the car washing her paw.

"The parlor? Where is the parlor? Wait, there's a dead person in there?"

"The parlor is on the third floor. And yes, as I already said, there is a dead guy up there." Jezebel was much sassier than I'd imagined, and she seemed pretty feisty before she started talking.

"Okay. Do you know who it was?" I asked.

"Some guy your Aunt brought in to fix something or other. It's not like I'd met him personally."

"You're a bit of a wise crack, aren't you?"

"Look, lady, you ask the questions, and I'm giving you straight answers. What more do you want?" Jez said and jumped down from the hood of the car.

"I'd like to know who the dead guy in my Aunt's bed and breakfast is?" I said and followed behind her.

"Fair enough." She said and swaggered towards the building.

Jezebel led me around to a cellar door behind the inn. I thought it was weird at first, but it did help me, and my talking cat, avoid the crowd out front.

I pulled the basement door open, and the loud creak it produced made me cringe. I really didn't want the rubberneckers up front to hear it and come running, but fortunately, they didn't.

Seven concrete steps descended into what appeared to be a dark, dank basement. I walked down the stairs and then stood on the third step with my arms stretched over my head holding the door open.

"Come on lady, we haven't got all day," Jezebel said while twitching her tail in annoyance.

"If I let it close any farther, it's going to make that terrible screeching sound again. It might draw their attention this time." I retorted.

"So, you're just going to stand there all day like that. You look like a giant, confused monkey." Jezebel turned around, sat down, and started staring at me in that judgmental way only cats can pull off.

"I doubt you even know what a monkey looks like. Not a real one, anyway."

"That's not the point." She said and started bathing her ears with her paw.

"You're not helping."

"Lady, I'm a cat. We don't help. But, if you're really this hopeless, you could always try a spell." Now she was glaring at me.

My arms were really starting to hurt, and I was beginning to forget why it mattered if the door creaked when I shut it. Even if people came to the house, the door would be closed, locked, and there'd be nothing to see. Then it hit me, my talking cat just told me to cast a spell.

"What do you mean a spell?" I asked, and now I was too intrigued to just close the cellar door.

"I'll explain more when you're not standing there looking like the sad goal posts of the losing football team. For now, try telling the door to be quiet when you close it and see what happens." Jezebel got up and started walking further into the cellar.

I looked up at the door, I now desperately wanted to be closed, and said, "Be quiet door."

It worked.

I quickly latched the door and tried to follow Jezebel into the basement. It was very dark, though, and I ran into a pile of baskets.

"Now try turning on the lights before you kill yourself." I heard Jez's snarky voice from the middle of the room.

"How am I supposed to find the switch?" I asked as I tried to pick up the baskets and restack them in the pitch black.

"You really are hopeless. I swear I don't know how you humans make it through the day without walking out in front of a truck." I could hear her tail swishing to the beat of her exasperation. "Try telling the lights to turn on, genius."

"Turn on lights?" Nothing. "Please."

The lights came on, and it took a few moments for my eyes to adjust. I looked around and took in the fascinating array of objects stored down in the cellar. In addition to the woven baskets I'd toppled, there was a vast selection of antique furniture, what looked like vintage clothing stored in plastic garment bags, and shelves full of candles, crystals, and tiny bottles. The far wall also had a door that said *Wine* in ornate lettering.

I walked over to one of the shelves and touched a huge block of what appeared to be black obsidian. "What is all of this stuff?"

"That looks like a bunch of rocks and candles." A man's voice made me jump halfway out of my skin.

I whirled around, and there was a man in coveralls standing behind me. Well, it wasn't really a man. It was more like the projection of a person. That's the best way I can describe it. He was only partly there, and he appeared to be transparent.

"Oh, sorry. Didn't mean to scare you, Ma'am." He said and floated towards me. "Although, I guess I am a little frightening."

"It's alright. Who are you?" I asked trying to act casual.

"He's the dead guy," Jezebel said. "Saw him with my own eyes upstairs."

"I'm dead?" The apparition asked. "Cats can talk? Have they always been able to speak?"

"Not all of us can talk. I'm special." Jezebel said proudly. "And yes, you're about as dead as they come."

"What's your name?" I had asked the ghost before he had the chance to respond to Jezebel's snark.

"I'm Lester Crumbly. I mean, I was Lester Crumbly. I guess I still am…" He trailed off as if lost in thought.

"You're still you. I'm sure of it. You're just disembodied." I tried to reassure him.

I had no experience with the dead. Well, no direct experience. I'd seen and felt things all my life that I couldn't explain, but this was my first face to face conversation with a dead person.

"How did I die?" He asked with wide eyes.

"I don't know," I answered.

"Stabbed in the back while you were changing the lightbulbs in the parlor," Jezebel said flatly. "What? I happened to walk by the body, your body, after the murder. I'm assuming you didn't stick the knife in your own back." She continued after Lester and I both stared at her.

"Do you know who killed you?" I asked hopefully.

"How would he know who killed him if he doesn't even remember how he died?" Jezebel mocked.

"Hush cat. Let him speak." I said, and she hissed at me softly.

"The last thing I remember was climbing up the step ladder to change one of the bulbs. I was just about done screwing it in, and I heard someone walk up behind me. I think." Lester said.

He stretched his hands out in front of him and wiggled his transparent fingers. It was as if he was still trying to take it all in. I don't blame him. I'd be completely shocked too.

"Do you remember anything else?" I asked.

"Oh, wait. They said something." Lester appeared to be digging deep in his memory, and Jezebel and I leaned forward in anticipation. "They said, *This is for*... And then I was down here with you guys."

"There's a bit of a time lapse there, dead guy," Jezebel said and yawned as if she'd grown bored with our conversation with the other side.

"I've been a ghost for like what? An hour now. What do you want from me? At least I'm not a cat."

That made me giggle. The dead guy had some spunk. I mean, Mr. Crumbly had some spunk.

Six

The ghost of Mr. Lester Crumbly didn't remember anything else, and then he vanished. So, Jezebel and I made our way upstairs to the main floor of the inn. The lobby and the breakfast room were completely empty, so I made my way quietly upstairs to the third floor.

I wasn't quite sure what I was doing, but that's where Jezebel headed, so I followed her. Once I was on the top floor, I could hear my Aunt talking to a man down the hall in what I assumed was the parlor. They were discussing the logistics of getting the body out of the bed and breakfast without having to contend with the crowd gathering out front.

The man said that the group wouldn't be too big as long as it was only gawkers from Tree's Hollow gathered outside. My Aunt countered that word had traveled fast and that people from surrounding towns had started to show up.

"The Coroner is almost here. I'm going to go out front and try to clear a path for him. That seems like the easiest thing to do." The man's voice said.

"Okay. Thankfully all of the guests have either checked out already or are out sightseeing." Aunt Kara responded.

At that point, I turned and went back downstairs to the second floor. I presumed the male voice was the Sheriff, and I didn't want him to find me eavesdropping.

Jezebel followed me, and we stood quietly outside my room while I decided what to do next. I was about to go into my room when Jezebel spoke up with a plan.

"You should go up there. Nobody is around. You could investigate."

"I should go poke around the parlor where the dead body is?" I ask her skeptically.

"His name is Lester Crumbly. You met him, remember?" Jezebel said and started walking back down the hall towards the stairs.

"You never know. You might help solve the murder. Wouldn't that be exciting, and at the very least, you'll have an excellent first story for your new job. Congratulations, by the way." She said.

"Thank you." I was touched by her moment of kindness.

Instead of arguing with Jezebel, I decided to follow her up the stairs to the third floor. She was right, and there was nobody up there. Even the crime scene tape that had been strung across the doorway to the parlor had fallen halfway off.

I stopped outside for a minute and contemplated whether I should go in. I was fairly sure that it was illegal to just walk into a crime scene and start poking around, but then again, earlier today I cast a spell, talked to a dead guy in the basement, and had more than one conversation with my talking cat.

Looking around the room, I could see why Aunt Kara called someone in to change the light bulbs. Even with the ones Lester had replaced, over half of them were out. I'd have to ask her why she didn't employ a full-time handyman.

Lester, or what was Lester, was lying on the carpet at the base of his stepladder. Sure enough, he'd been stabbed. I diverted my eyes from him right away. I might be an investigative reporter now, but that's not something I wanted to oogle for a long time.

My fear of walking into the room and destroying the crime scene vanished when Jezebel trotted into the room. "Come on." She said as she swished past me. "What are you, a chicken?"

I took two steps into the room and immediately noticed the smell of lily of the valley. It reminded me of a perfume I used to wear in junior high. Over on an end table, I spotted a cell phone. Curious as to whether it belonged to Lester, I walked over and picked it up.

To my relief, it wasn't locked by password. I taped the home icon and immediately noticed that Lester had a couple of unanswered text messages.

Those messages, along with most of the others, painted a very distinct picture of Lester Crumbly. I read a few of them and realized that he was fortunate that he was the only handyman in town because Lester was not well liked.

Most of the messages were about him being absurdly late and ruining people's plans. I also read many angry texts about overcharging and poor customer service.

"He wasn't well liked," I said to Jezebel and set the phone back down.

"Ya think?"

"Well, yeah, obviously somebody didn't like him," I said and motioned towards the body without looking at it. "But, what I mean is that it appears that nobody really liked him."

Before Jezebel could respond, I heard my Aunt Kara and the Sheriff coming back up the stairs.

"Oh no," I whispered.

"Through here," Jezebel said and walked over to the wall.

She rubbed up against what looked like a regular wall, but when Jez bumped it with her head, I heard a faint clicking. I walked over and pushed gently on the space.

The secret door opened up, and I found myself in a hidden passageway within the walls. I quickly closed the panel and looked around for Jezebel. She was making her way down the short passage, so I followed close behind her.

"How did you know this was here?" I whispered once I knew we were clear of the parlor. "Was it magic? Are you a witch too?"

"I felt the draft coming from the door. I guess at one time it was hermetically sealed, but it's an old house now. As far as your question about me being a witch, let me ask you a question. Have you ever even watched a show or movie about witches? What about books? Surely you must have read a book with a witch in it."

"Not really my genre. I mean, I'm sure I've seen or read something, but I probably didn't pay much attention." I answered as we walked down a narrow staircase.

"Not really your genre. Lady, you are too funny, and so is the goddess for sticking me with you." She stopped in at the bottom of the staircase and sat down.

"You're mean."

"Thank you. I try, ya know. Anyway, I'm your familiar. If you don't know what that is because you grew up under a rock, I suggest you look it up on the internet." She said and head-butted the wall again.

Another faint clicking.

"Wait, this is our room," I said as I passed through the opening and shut the panel behind us.

"Very observant. I find it ironic that I'm a cat that knows about the internet and you're a witch that didn't know about your familiar." Jezebel said and hopped up on the bed. "While you're looking up familiars, why don't you use Google to find the dead man's address? You could go poke around his house."

"You want me to trespass at a murder victim's house?

"Either that or you could lie down and take a nap with me. Maybe your story will write itself." She said and rolled over on her back. "But, lady, before you go, could you rub my belly."

I still had the keys to Aunt Kara's car, so I snuck out through the cellar door. I was worried that I'd see Lester's ghost again, but I didn't. Besides, why should I be scared of him? We'd already met.

The cellar door was unlocked when Jezebel led me down there, so I figured it wouldn't hurt too much to leave it unlocked again. I didn't plan on being gone long, and I'd make sure to latch it again when I got back. It wasn't a good idea to leave it open like that.

It was important that I get away from all of the hubbub to do my research, so I pulled Kara's car out of the lot and drove down the road. Within a few miles, I found the picnic area that I'd passed on my way to the job interview earlier in the day. There wasn't any Wi-Fi in the area, so I turned my phone into a hotspot and hoped for the best.

The internet crawled out here because of the forest, but I was still able to use Google to find Lester Crumbly's address. He had several social media accounts too, but it looked like he'd stopped posting on them a long time ago when a flood of negative posts hit them.

I closed my laptop, put it in the passenger seat, and plugged the address into the GPS. Lester's house was on the outskirts of town if you could even call it that. The turnoff for his place must have been almost a mile outside of the Tree's Hollow town limits, and after I had turned onto his driveway, I found myself driving deep into the woods.

Lester's cabin was small. It's metal roof looked like it was in desperate need of some attention. As did his front door and windows. In fact, it didn't appear that a handyman lived in the house at all. I got back online and checked the address. I was in the right place, so I got out of the car and started to walk around to the back of the house.

There didn't appear to be any police around. I guess that should have been obvious since there wasn't a cruiser in the driveway. If something happened and they had shown up, I would have sworn that I was just new in town and got lost.

I wasn't sure how far that story would get me considering I was snooping around a murder victim's house, but it was the best I could come up with at the time. The truth was that I was more nervous than I'd ever been in my entire life. My heart was pounding out of my chest, and a cold line of sweat was running down my back. A breeze kicked up out of nowhere, and it gave me chills.

I stopped at a small window on the side of the cabin, stood up on the tips of my toes, and tried to peek inside. The inside of the cabin was dark, but since the sun was starting to hang low in the sky outside, it actually helped me see inside the house.

The cabin was small and sparsely furnished. The living room, dining area, and kitchen were all one big room. There were only two doors off the main room, and I assumed those were the bathroom and bedroom. I surveyed the room for signs of foul play but then reminded myself that he was murdered at the inn.

My calves started to ache from holding me up, so I stopped looking in the side window and walked around to the back. The rear door to the cabin was closed, but curiosity got the better of me, and I reached out to turn the knob.

"Can I help you with something?" A deep male voice asked from behind me.

I yelped, or squeaked, and let go of the knob. At first, I wasn't sure what to do, so I just stood there as still as I could manage and hoped that he'd go away.

"I can see you, ya know. No matter how much you try to ignore me." He said with a chuckle.

The sound of his laugh brought a smile to my face despite the fact that I was trying to break into a dead man's house. I clenched and unclenched my hands a couple of times while taking deep breaths.

I was hoping to prepare myself for this confrontation, but it became abundantly clear that my only choice was just to turn around and face the music.

I turned around and tried to apologize, but the words got stuck in my throat. I'd lived in a city with at least a million men, and I'd never seen one like this before. He took a step towards me, and I squeaked again.

Ranger McDreamy was standing in front of me in all of his six-foot-two glory looking every inch the rugged Norse god I suddenly imagined he was. His blue eyes sparkled in the fading afternoon sun, and his strong, square jaw was covered with the perfect amount of stubble.

I rubbed my cheek reflexively when I thought about it brushing against my face. I had to have been about a half of a second away from drooling all over myself when he spoke again.

"Ma'am, are you okay?" He asked.

"Uh huh." But, honestly, I was still mesmerized by the way his Ranger's uniform fit him just right.

"Ma'am?"

"Oh, sorry. Yeah, uh. I'm uh. Hi there." I said and smiled at him.

"Is there something I can help you with? Are you looking for Mr. Crumbly?"

"No, not looking for him."

"I didn't think so. It's customary to use the front door." He said and took another step towards me.

I suppressed the squeak that time, but my brain wouldn't engage to help me come up with a reason for being there snooping around a dead man's house.

"Are you going to make me guess why you're here or are you just going to tell me?" He continued.

I could hear hints of both amusement and impatience in his voice. Once I was able to pull my gaze away from his biceps, I started to formulate coherent thoughts again.

"Are you going to tell me why a Forest Ranger is in Lester's back yard?" I used his first name as if I knew him to add an air of authority to my question.

"You know, only guilty people and lawyers answer questions with a question." He smirked at me impishly.

Was he bantering with me?

"I'm neither of those things," I said with a shy smile. "Well, I suppose I'm guilty of snooping." Something about this man makes the truth spill out of me in a way I didn't expect. "I'm Lenny Brewer, the newest investigative reporter for the Tree's Hollow Tribune."

I extended my hand to him and flashed Ranger McDreamy my best, *please don't call the cops on me* smile. He took my hand and shook it firmly, but what caught me off guard was the feeling of electrical current that ran between us.

"It's a pleasure to meet you, Ms. Brewer. I'm Nathan Carter. I'm a ranger." He said and let go of my hand.

"Oh, really? I thought maybe you were an astronaut." At this point, I really hoped he was bantering earlier.

"Well, I thought you were a thief, but it turns out you're just trespassing," Nathan said completely stone-faced.

"Oh gosh. I mean, I wasn't trying to break the law or anything." I stammered.

"Whoa, it's okay." He said with his hands up in front of him in surrender. "I was just teasing you. Sorry. You're as white as I've ever seen a person turn."

Seven

"I suppose the proper thing to do is to call the Sheriff seeing as how you're snooping around a murder victim's house before the police have even had the chance to search the place, but somehow that doesn't seem right. They'll never solve the case, you know." Nathan said.

"So, that means I have two questions for you," I said hoping to keep the conversation off calling the police.

"Well, go on."

For a moment, I'm stunned. I can't believe that he's actually letting me engage him in a conversation. There's a post holding up the awning over the back porch, and he leans against it. I lose my train of thought for a moment because I'd never seen a man lean up against a pole quite the way Nathan did. I managed to shake it off before he asked me if I was okay again.

"The first question is that I'm wondering what a forest ranger is doing in a murder victim's back yard."

"Mr. Crumbly's land borders the woods. I drop in and say hello sometimes when my patrol brings me close." Nathan answered. "What about your second question?"

I didn't get the chance to ask Nathan another question. His radio crackled and came to life. He'd gotten a call about a hiker with a broken ankle and had to leave.

"Meet me tonight at the coffee house on the square." He said just before he left.

Nathan didn't wait for an answer, but that's okay because I would have said yes. I probably would have agreed a little too enthusiastically, so his hasty departure saved me from embarrassing myself again.

When I was just about to abandon my search, my luck turned for the worse. My hand was on the car door handle when the Sherriff's cruiser pulled in behind my car.

"I'm going to need you to come with me, Ma'am."

It was just my luck that another tall, ruggedly handsome man wanted my attention today. Sherriff Hanson was almost as tall as Nathan was, but he had dark, wavy hair and big friendly brown eyes.

Fortunately, I didn't feel the same vibe with him as I did with Nathan. That would have made my life unbearably complicated. Sheriff Hanson, Brad, was easy to look at, though, and it did make my interrogation a bit more interesting.

Brad let me follow him to the County Sherriff's office instead of taking me in his car. It was a few miles away, and I used the drive to calm my nerves. Apparently, none of the towns in Hardin County had their own police departments anymore, and now Sheriff Hanson and a few deputies had to protect and serve the entire area.

I guessed that was why Nathan said they'd never solve the murder, and it wasn't because he was indicating that Brad and his deputies were incompetent.

You never know, though.

The police department's building was small. Brad led me through an office area with a few desks to the only interrogation room. It didn't look like the ones I'd seen in the movies at all.

There was another desk with two chairs near the back wall of the room. Right inside the door was a small red sofa, fake wood coffee table, and a worn easy chair. It was all very comfortable and shabby chic.

Brad gestured towards the sofa and said: "Have a seat."

He sat down on the chair and set a recording device down on the pre-fab coffee table. Brad rattled off the date and a bunch of other jargon as he started recording. I probably should have been paying attention, but I was too busy looking around the room.

The walls were decorated with old movie posters in gold frames. At first, I wondered how safe it was to have something that could be used as a weapon hanging on the walls, but then I realized they were most likely nailed down tight.

"Are you ready to begin, Ms. Brewer?" Brad said.

He over-enunciated my name for the recording, and it almost made me laugh. I caught the giggle just in time. At this point, I wasn't sure if I was a suspect or they were just gathering information. I probably should have picked up on the fact that I was in an interrogation room, but it went right over my head at the time.

"Sure," I said, and then the weight of the situation hit me. "Uh, am I under arrest?"

"Should you be?" Brad answered my question with a question, and I remembered what Nathan said about guilty people and lawyer. It made me smile.

"No. I shouldn't be. I would like to help, though. I'm not really sure how much I can do for you right now. I don't know anything about Lester's death."

"You call him Lester like you knew him. That seems odd given how new you are in town. It's also peculiar that you were poking around his house before the police even had a chance to search the place." Brad said and leaned toward me.

"I didn't know him at all. I just moved here, and I only called him by name because I found it on the internet. Sorry. What I meant was that I don't know anything about Mr. Crumbly's death." I was suddenly filled with righteous indignation over Sheriff Hanson's accusations.

"I understand." He softened considerably. "Did you see anything at his place? Anything I should know about?"

"No, not really. A forest ranger came upon me while I was investigating and interrupted me." I said thoughtfully. "I got back to the inn after he was already dead. I didn't see anybody around. In fact, I didn't even see you or my Aunt Kara. I only heard your voices. Then, I left for Lester's place."

"If you didn't see me, how do you know I was there?" Brad asked. He pulled a notepad and pen out of his jacket pocket.

"As I said, I heard your voice. It was you, wasn't it?"

"It was. So, you said that a forest ranger found you trespassing on Mr. Crumbly's property. Can you tell me the name of the ranger?"

This guy was really getting my hackles up. He was so smug and accusatory, and I wasn't quite sure how to take that. There was no reason to believe I'd killed the man. Sure, I was new in town, and I'd been investigating his house, but I had no reason to stab a man in the back while he changed lightbulbs.

"His name was Nathan Carter," I answered as cordially as I could.

"That's what I thought. What I can't fathom is why he didn't call me when he caught you trespassing." Brad said and scratched his temple with the end of his pen.

"I wasn't trespassing. I was investigating. I'm an investigative reporter." I said impatiently.

"Oh really? So, would you mind showing me your press credentials, then?"

I must have turned about fifty shades of red. I was sure Charles would get my credentials for me, but I didn't have them yet. To anyone but my new boss, I just looked like some snoopy crackpot.

"I don't have them yet. But, you can call my new boss, Charles Zapier, and I'm sure he'll vouch for me." I mumbled.

"You know, I believe you. The problem is that you can't just trespass and call it an investigation. Do we have an understanding?"

"We do," I responded.

"And, if you do find anything out that could help with the actual police investigation, you're going to bring that information to me." He said sternly. "Right?"

Right then, any attraction I felt to Sherriff Stickuphisbutt vanished. He was still handsome, but all of a sudden, it felt like I was in the presence of a very stern and frustratingly annoying big brother.

"Fine." I crossed my fingers behind my back when I said this, so it wasn't technically a lie.

Sherriff Brad Stickuphisbutt gave me his business card and offered to drive me back to the inn. I told him I had my car, but I ended up having to insist that I could drive myself.

On the drive back to town, I reflected on my first day in Tree's Hollow. I stopped in at the inn to change clothes for my coffee date with Nathan.

Jezebel was in our room waiting for dinner, which I fed her dutifully before I searched through my suitcases for something suitable to wear.

I didn't want to overdress and come off as desperate, so I settled on a black sweater, jeans, and my favorite black boots.

"Why don't you come over here and sit down for a moment." Jezebel teased as soon as I pulled on the black sweater.

"In your dreams cat."

"You won't be out too late, will you?" She said and hopped up on the mini fridge next to the television stand.

"I'm just having coffee with a new friend. I'll be home in plenty of time for an early bedtime, and I'm touched that you miss me." I said and patted her head.

"Lady, I'm don't miss you. I wanted to make sure you were here in time for my bedtime snack." Jezebel said and jumped down.

With a shake of my head and a sigh, I left the room. I know Jez wanted to wander the halls, but there were guests around, so I locked the door behind me. She knew how to open the panels to the secret passages, so I figured she could explore inside the walls if she got too restless.

I stopped downstairs in the breakfast room and asked Aunt Kara if I could use her car again. The inn hosts a cocktail and appetizer hour for guests. It would usually be held in the parlor, according to the flyer in my room, but I guess due to the murder they were holding it downstairs tonight.

"Of course you can take the car. I'm in for the evening. Not that I go too many places. Who are you meeting?" She asked, but I could tell by the twinkle in her eye that Aunt Kara already knew.

The Coffee Cabal looked like most of the other trendy coffee houses I'd visited in the city, but somehow the atmosphere was different. No one sitting at the smattering of tables was on their phone or a laptop, and there were several small groups of people having quiet conversations.

I walked in and stood back from the counter studying the menu while I waited for Nathan to arrive. The menu looked fairly standard with a variety of different hot and cold drinks. I was delighted to see that they had my favorite, iced chai, on the menu.

"I vote we order coffee." Nathan practically appeared next to me.

"I prefer tea. Chai to be exact."

"Black coffee for me. The darker, the better. Do you want that Chai hot or iced?" He said before stepping up to the counter. "I'm going to guess iced."

"You'd be correct." Him knowing what I like to drink made me smile like a silly school girl.

I was going to have to be careful, or I might end up falling for Ranger McDreamy. He paid for our drinks and then led us to an empty table near the windows. The insides of the window frames were lined with what looked like Christmas lights in the shape of chili peppers. The glow gave the place a magical feel that you only noticed when you were seated at a table.

Nathan took a sip of his coffee and let out a satisfied sigh. "I don't think I've ever had coffee with a real writer before." He said before taking another drink.

"That's hard to believe. You had to go to college to be a forest ranger, right?"

"I did, but I don't recall having any writer friends. None as pretty as you, anyway. I'd remember that for sure." He said with a wicked smile.

"Oh, now flattery will get you everywhere with me."

It's a good thing that Chai doesn't have much caffeine in it because we sat there together long enough for me to drink three of them. We talked about college, our families, and our careers. When it was time to go home, he walked me to my car and kissed me on the cheek.

"Can I give you my phone number?" He asked more shyly than I expected.

Of course, I said yes, and he recited the number as I put it into my phone.

"Text me when you get back to the inn, and let me know you made it home okay," Nathan said as I got into my car.

I couldn't believe I'd met someone so wonderful my first day in my new town. I was glad he didn't bring up the murder, but I guessed we'd have to talk about it eventually.

The past two days had seen a dramatic shift in my life. All of it hit me as I was pulling into the parking lot of the bed and breakfast. I needed to sleep on everything.

When I got inside, I gave Jezebel her evening snack. I found another pair of pajamas in my bags and got ready for bed. Jezebel ate quickly and then snuggled into the bed beside me.

"Night, lady."

"Night, cat."

It was then that I realized I'd left all the lights on. But, that wasn't a problem for me anymore. Was it?

"Lights out."

Nothing…

"Please?"

A satisfied smile crossed my face as the room went blissfully dark.

Eight

The next morning I woke up, ate breakfast, gave Jezebel her cream, and got ready for work in record time. I was in a hurry to get to the paper and tell Charles everything that had happened.

It was terrible that someone was murdered, but I thought that perhaps I could help solve the crime and impress my new boss with my very first story. I was not at all prepared for how Charles was actually going to react.

I got into the office, made some coffee, and then sat down at my desk with my shiny new laptop. Inspiration hit, so I was clicking away furiously at the keys when Charles finally looked up from what he was doing and acknowledged that I was there.

"You seem enthusiastic today. What have you got?" There was a pitch of apprehension in his voice that I didn't expect.

"Working on a story about the murder at my Aunt's place," I said without looking up from my laptop screen.

"Oh, dear. I thought that might be the case. I'm just wondering if maybe you should go for something a little more light-hearted for your first story." Charles said.

That did make me stop typing. I felt all of the confidence I'd built up over the last couple of days run out of me like water through a sieve.

"I thought this would be an excellent way to show off my investigative reporting skills. It's also huge news, so won't people think it's strange if the only local paper doesn't cover the story?" I asked hopefully.

"I have to go. I have a doctor's appointment. You can stay as long as you like, but I would encourage you to consider another story."

And then, Charles was out the door. Not knowing anything about this town or why the Editor-in-Chief of the local paper would get emotional about the death of a widely disliked handyman got my curiosity up.

I took out my phone and gave Nathan a call. I wanted to bounce all of this information off someone, but I also wanted an excuse to talk to him.

"Where are you?" I asked when he picked up.

"Well, hello to you too."

"Sorry, that was rude. Hi, Nathan. It's Lenny. How are you today?" I asked.

"I'm good, thank you. How are you?" I could hear the smile on his face in his voice.

"Pretty good. Thank you for asking. Now, where are you?"

"Haha. You're hilarious." Nathan laughed.

After some back and forth banter about how he was in the woods, he happily agreed to meet me. Nathan said that he was close to Lester Crumbly's place again, and I said I'd be right there.

When I pulled into Lester's driveway, there was a green jeep parked in the driveway. The vehicle had a National Park's logo on it, but it did not have a handsome forest ranger inside.

I got out of the car and went around to the back of the cabin, but there was still no sign of Nathan. It made me incredibly nervous that there had just been a murder, and now the person I wanted to talk about the crime with seemed to have vanished. I was just about to panic when I noticed there was a path at the end of Lester's yard that led into a wooded area.

The trail was short, and it went to a small clearing with a picnic table. Nathan was sitting at the table writing in a notebook. I fought the urge to walk up and hug him from behind. Everything about him made me feel comfortable and familiar, but I wanted to avoid looking desperately crazy too soon.

"Hello," I said.

"Hi, Lenny," Nathan said as he stood up from the bench. "I figured you'd be a few more minutes. You must have a lead foot. Anyway, sorry I wasn't up there waiting for you in the driveway."

"It's okay, and you're right. I should probably start obeying the speed limits instead of viewing them as a suggestion." I snortled at my own joke and then felt my cheeks turn bright red.

Nathan started laughing too, and I felt relieved. The relief was short lived. We both turned our attention up the path towards the house as we heard the door to the cabin slam shut. The next sound was that of a car door slamming and tires squealing as whoever it was backed out of the driveway by putting the gas pedal to the floor.

"What the heck?" Nathan said, and he took off running towards the house.

I chase after him, but by the time we make it back up the path, the car is gone. That's when I notice that there is a piece of paper stuck to the door with a knife. The sight of it makes my blood run cold because now I know that not only am I being followed, whoever is following me is trying to scare me too.

"Stay here," Nathan says firmly and then walks towards the door.

I watch him lean over a bit and read the note without pulling the knife out of the door. He shakes his head and then heads back over to where I'm standing.

"What did it say?" I ask, but I'm not entirely sure that I want to know the answer.

"It said to be careful, or someone would be reporting your death next." Nathan practically growled as he spoke the words. "I have to call this in to Sheriff Hanson. He's probably going to be peeved that we're here again, but I still have to tell him."

"Yeah." Was all I could muster.

Nathan took my hand and held it until we saw Brad's cruiser pulling up the driveway. The Sheriff looked upset, and he held a hand up to us as we started walking towards him.

"You two stay right there." He said.

Brad read the note and then got an evidence bag out of his car. I watched him slip on a pair of gloves and then wiggle the knife free from the door. He put the note in a separate bag that was stuck to the back of the first.

I didn't like the expression on his face as he walked towards Nathan and me, and I wished that Nate was still holding my hand. I took a deep breath and tried to push down the bad feeling that was bubbling up inside of me like acid.

"This knife came from the same set as the one that killed Lester Crumbly," Brad said grimly.

"That means that she's in danger," Nathan responded as he protectively took a half step in front of me.

"She was in danger. I'm sure she'll be okay now. This incident gives me what I need to arrest my number one suspect." Brad wouldn't look me in the eyes as he said this.

"Well that's good, right?" Nate countered.

"Look, normally I wouldn't tell you guys this as this is still an active investigation, but I feel bad letting Lenora get blindsided." Now Brad was looking right at me, and I realized that I liked it better when he was watching his shoes. The look in his eyes gave me chills. "The knives came from a set at the inn. Normally that wouldn't mean too much, but this particular set was stored in a place that only Kara had access to."

"Aunt Kara?" I felt like I was going to be sick.

"I'm sorry," Was all Brad had said before he turned to leave.

The bile rising up in my throat threatened to choke me. My vision started to close in just as white starbursts started going off in front of my eyes. It felt like I couldn't take a deep breath, and the last thing I remember was a pair of strong arms catching me as I fell.

When the world started to come back into focus, it became apparent very quickly that I was in the hospital. The antiseptic smell was overpowering, and I could feel the burning and stabbing sensation of the IV needle in my arm.

My first inclination was to claw at it and get it out of my skin, but I resisted. I could hear the beeping of a monitor right next to me, and I could hear several more in the distance. I looked around the room as my vision started to clear, and I was happy to see Nathan sitting in a chair with his notebook.

I watched him for a couple of minutes before I said anything, and I discovered that he wasn't writing at all. He was drawing. It almost looked like Nathan was bringing a picture of a leaf to life with his lines and shading.

"Did you call my Aunt Kara?" I stretched, and I'd apparently forgotten everything that happened before I passed out.

"Lenny, you're awake," Nathan said.

He got up and came over to my bedside. His eyes looked troubled as he gently brushed a strand of my hair off my forehead.

"Did Brad arrest my Aunt?"

"I'm afraid so," Nate said.

"Nathan, she didn't do this. Aunt Kara didn't kill anybody." I tried to sit up, but I felt woozy.

"Whoa, Lenny. Try to relax. The nurse said that you're dehydrated and your blood sugar was low. That's why you've got an IV."

I tried to think back over the last couple of days. I knew that I'd eaten, but I guess I hadn't been paying attention to how little. I'd rushed this morning and only had a banana and half of a carton of chocolate milk. I couldn't remember eating anything but breakfast yesterday, either. Normally, I'm not the kind of person who forgets to eat.

Ever.

"I'm sorry. I hope you're not getting yourself in trouble with work by being here." I said and rubbed at the spot where the IV went into my arm.

"You don't have to be sorry, but you do need to take better care of yourself. Your IV bags are almost empty. Now that you're awake, hopefully, the doctors will let me get you out of here. We're going straight to Tilly's Table and getting you a proper meal."

I started to protest, but Nate was right. If I was going to help Aunt Kara, I needed to take care of myself. I wasn't any good to her if I let the stress drag me so far down that I ended up in the hospital getting IV fluids.

"Okay, but then I have to figure out how to help my Aunt," I said as Nathan handed me my shoes.

"I'll help any way that I can. I am at your service." Nate said and gave me a little bow.

I really appreciated him trying to cheer me up, and I was grateful for the help too. My doctor discharged me a half an hour later after Nathan promised to take me to eat as soon as we left.

He drove us to Tilly's Table on the other side of Tree's Hollow. The lunch rush was starting to leave, and there were only a couple of tables occupied inside the cozy restaurant.

The smell of cooking food made my stomach grumble audibly. I couldn't believe how hungry I'd let myself get. We sat down, and I grabbed a menu out of the condiment/menu holder. I was happy to see that Tilly's served breakfast all day, and it took me about five seconds to settle on French toast with eggs and bacon. Nathan ordered blueberry pancakes with sausage, and I made a mental note to order that the next time I ate here.

"I don't know where to start with exonerating Aunt Kara," I said mournfully after the server took our orders.

"I guess that if they arrested her, she didn't have a solid enough alibi. So, we probably need to find a way to prove that someone else had access to the knives." Nathan said as he folded his napkin into the shape of a bird.

Nine

The food at Tilly's was delicious, and I felt much stronger after I got my belly full. Nathan needed to go check in at work, so he took me back to my car and promised to pick me up for dinner.

"I've got to make sure you're eating. It's my gentlemanly duty." He said before kissing me on the cheek again.

Once he was gone, I realized that I was alone with Lester's house again. The temptation to try the back door was too strong to resist, so I figured I'd have a look around.

As I turned the knob, part of me wished it wouldn't open. No such luck. The doorknob clicked, and I was able to push it open. I stepped inside the house, and I was relieved that the dread I'd anticipated feeling never showed up.

Lenny Brewer is not afraid of a little breaking and entering. Okay, so I didn't exactly do any breaking, but I was still feeling pretty bold about my secret mission. I searched through the living room first, and the only interesting thing I found was an Egyptian Book of the Dead in the coffee table drawer.

It was only interesting because I'd never read it and it seemed out of place. My intuition told me it didn't have anything to do with the murder, so I shut the drawer and decided to order a copy of the book when I got home.

There was some high blood pressure medication in the bathroom cabinet, but for the most part, the rest of Lester's house was completely unremarkable. I checked the knife block in the kitchen, and all of them were present and accounted for.

In Lester's bedroom, I found a box of unsent letters to Constance Piper. I opened one up to see why Mr. Crumbly had written a bunch of letters to the old advice columnist. To my surprise, they were love letters. I considered sitting here reading them, but that was completely impractical.

I made the decision to take the box of letters with me. I was already guilty of breaking and entering and trespassing, I figured it wouldn't hurt to add burglary to my rap sheet.

Nick was working the desk at the bed and breakfast by the time I got back, and he looked like he was about to become unhinged. He asked me a hundred different ways if I knew what was going on with Aunt Kara, but I didn't have any answers for him yet.

I'd stopped at the market on my way home and picked up some canned cat food for Jezebel. It was some sort of tuna feast that I figured she'd like. I was right, and she gobbled it down while I read a few of the letters.

"Your boss came by the inn today," Jezebel said as she licked the last of her food out of the can.

"He did? When?"

"He was in here a little while before Sherriff Brad came in and arrested Kara," Jezebel said, and then she sniffed the can for any morsel of food she'd forgotten.

"Wait, how do you know the person was my boss? You've never seen him before."

"Kara called him Charles, that's your boss's name, and he said he wanted to talk to her about writing an article about the inn's history. I put two and two together, lady. God, you act like I'm a dog or something."

"It's not nice to say dogs are stupid." I chastised.

"At least I didn't say you were stupid." Jezebel ran into the bathroom before I could respond.

The unsent letters were all earnestly written declarations of love. Although they weren't exactly poetry, I could tell how much affection Lester had for Constance. I began to wonder why he never sent them and if she knew about his feelings for her. I searched through the box, but there weren't any letters from Constance to Lester.

I had the box of "Dear Constance" letters that Charles had given me, and I started to wonder if there was anything helpful in there. I looked through the box, but there were hundreds of envelopes. It was going to take me forever to go through them all unless I found a way to narrow them down.

"Hey, cat," I called into the bathroom.

"What?" Jezebel responded without coming out.

"Can I use my magic to say… I don't know… Make someone more willing to talk to me?"

"You mean can you use your witch powers to mind control other sentient beings?" She snarked back at me.

"Well, when you say it that way it sounds so awful. I just want to make someone who doesn't know me a little more willing to open up to me in conversation." I responded sheepishly.

"You know, when you put it that way, it doesn't sound any better. But that doesn't matter because yes you can use your powers to get someone to spill their beans. Be careful how you use it, though. Magic has consequences." Jezebel's head peeked out of the bathroom.

"What do you mean?" That sounded terrifying, and I thought that maybe I should never use magic again.

"The Law of Three applies to everything you do," Jezebel said.

"The Law of Three?"

"Yeah. Goddess help me. You're hopeless. I'm not sure why the universe chose you to be a witch." Jez said and rolled over on her back.

"Just spill your beans, cat. Or, I'll have to use a little bit of my magic on you." I tried to sound menacing, but she looked too adorable.

"Whoa, lady. Nobody likes a salty witch. Anywhoo, whatever you use your powers for comes back to you times three. Whatever you put out into the world, the universe triples it and returns it to you. Three times the good and three times the bad. The goddess and the universe can't tell you how to use your power, but they can encourage you to use it for good."

I walked over to her and rubbed her belly. She only clawed me a little before finally starting to purr and then falling asleep. When the phone on the nightstand rang, it didn't even wake Jezebel up from her cat nap.

"There's a gentleman in the lobby to see you," Nick said. "He told me you have a dinner engagement."

"Tell him I'll be down in a few minutes, please," I responded.

Nick's only reply was to sigh loudly and then hang up the phone. My guess is that he was annoyed with me for going out on a dinner date while Aunt Kara was in jail.

I really wanted to talk to her because there was always the possibility that she knew something that could help, but I doubted that Brad would let me speak to her tonight. Tomorrow I was going to the Sherriff's station, and I would make a nuisance of myself until they let me see her.

Since I needed to get ready to go in a hurry, I threw on a black shirt, jeans, and my boots. Nathan was probably going to think it's my uniform, but that would have to be okay. I wanted to talk to him about the letters, and I also wanted to eat before the stress of Aunt Kara's arrest caught up with me. I knew if I thought about it too much, I'd lose my appetite.

Nathan took me one town over, and we ate sandwiches and chips at a deli. I told him about the letters, and he suggested that we go talk to Constance together.

"Do you think it's too late to drop in tonight?" I asked as I finished my chips.

"It's only seven. I know where she lives. If we drive by and the lights are off, we'll just keep going. But, if they're on, it won't hurt to at least ask if she's willing to talk to us."

"I want you to know that none of this is what I was expecting when I moved to Tree's Hollow. I thought things would be quieter down here." I said.

"Yeah, the forest has a particular energy. It's hard for me to put my finger on why it's so different here, but I know there is something that makes this entire area a little left of normal." He said with a shy smile.

If you only knew.

After we were done eating, Nathan drove us to Constance Piper's house. I was happy to see the lights were still on, but I was apprehensive about knocking on her door.

Nathan took my hand as we walked up the sidewalk to her wraparound porch. I felt a lot stronger with him at my side. My nerves were getting the better of me, and I couldn't bring myself to reach out and ring her doorbell, but Nate had me covered.

When Constance opened the door, Nathan introduced me and explained why we were there. It was then that I noticed her eyes were red like she'd been crying.

"Yes, please come in. Would you two like some coffee?" Constance said quietly.

Nathan and I sat down on the sofa, and I looked around the room while we waited for Constance to brew a pot of coffee. Almost the entire room looked like something straight out of the 1970's. I ran my hand over the lime green fabric of the sofa and pushed the burnt orange shag carpeting around with my toe.

There were wood shelves on the walls lined with kitschy knick knacks. The only thing that didn't fit was the sixty-five-inch flat screen television. It made me chuckle because the modern television was sitting on top of an old console TV.

I got up and went into the kitchen when I heard sobbing. Constance was standing in front of her coffee pot crying into a tissue. I ask her if she wanted us to go.

"No dear. I'll be okay. Besides, you're probably Lester's only chance for justice.

We spoke with Constance for over an hour. She and Lester had both been widowed for years, and they'd had a flirtation going for at least the last two.

Constance said the letters were never mailed because they passed them back and forth to each other. Apparently, Lester wrote them faster than he gave them to Connie. She went into another room and produced a box of similar letters that he'd given her over the last couple of years.

The one thing that was odd was that Connie told me there should have been a box of letters from her in Lester's house. Either he'd hidden them somewhere that I hadn't found them, or whoever killed Mr. Crumbly went into his house and stole the box.

"Do you have any idea who would want to kill Lester or steal your letters?" Nathan asked.

Ten

It turns out that while Connie was heartbroken, she was still a bit of a gossip. Nate asked her whom she thought killed Lester, and Constance had a long list of suspects. I picked up quickly that she understood how many people were annoyed with him for doing business the way he did, but Connie loved him anyway.

Unfortunately, her extensive list of suspects didn't put me any closer to knowing who killed Lester. I needed to find the box of letters that the killer stole, but how was I going to do that? I didn't know this town, and I hardly knew anyone who lived here. I was completely ill-prepared to solve a murder mystery this soon into my investigative reporting career.

I was about to have Nathan drive me home when my cell phone rang. I pulled it out of my pocket and looked at the screen. I didn't recognize the number, but my gut made me answer it anyway.

"Lenny? Lenny are you there?" Aunt Kara's voice.

"Aunt Kara, yeah, it's me. The police are letting you call me? Are you alright?" I tried not to panic.

"Brat, someone else was murdered. The killer used a knife from the same set that supposedly only I had access to, but I've been in jail. They're letting me go. Can you come pick me up?" Kara sounded like she was close to tears.

"Yes. I'm with Nathan Carter, but we'll be right there. We're going to come get you right now."

It felt like the drive to the county jail took forever. Aunt Kara was waiting out front for us when we pulled into the parking lot. She practically ran out to Nathan's car and jumped in.

He took us back to the inn and rented one of the vacant rooms. Nathan said there was no way he was leaving us alone while a killer was on the prowl. I have to admit that he was completely adorable when he tried to go alpha male on us.

I made coffee and we sat around one of the tables in the breakfast room sipping it. Aunt Kara looked extremely tired, and while I was relieved that she was home, I couldn't shake the feeling of dread.

I'd had no idea she was going to be arrested the first time, and it scared me to death that Sherriff Brad might come back for her at any moment. There was also the little problem of us being right in the center of a murder investigation.

As for me, I'd involved myself. Aunt Kara, on the other hand, didn't ask for any of this. I had to figure out who'd framed her soon so that none of us had to worry about her being carted off to jail again.

"I guess I should tell you who else died." Aunt Kara said.

Nathan and I leaned forward in anticipation. He grabbed my hand under the table and gave it a squeeze while I bit my bottom lip nervously.

"Who was it?" I asked

"They found David Fox in the bookstore bathroom with one of those knives in his back."

"That's the retired newspaper columnist." Nathan said, and I remembered Charles talking about him.

That was two people close to Constance Piper dead. She seemed so sad about Lester's death. Could it have been a ruse? It's entirely possible that Connie stole the letters from Lester's house to hide something in them.

"I need to go to the Tribune's office." I said and stood up.

"Why?" Nathan asked with wide eyes.

"All of the letters are in the same boxes. The ones to Constance and all of the letters I took to answer for the columns are in the same white file boxes with a purple stripe running around the center.

There are more of those boxes in the office. I have a hunch and, I just need to know for sure. I don't think Charles had anything to do with this, but I'll never forgive myself if I don't at least check it out."

"I'll take you. I don't want you going alone." Nathan said right before his phone rang.

He picked it up and walked away from us for a moment. His voice was hushed, and Nate kept running his hand through his thick hair nervously. "I'll be right there." I heard him say right before he disconnected.

"What is it?" Aunt Kara asked before I could get the words out.

"Lester Crumbly's house is on fire. The flames are spreading across his back yard towards the forest. The firefighters are on scene, but they want me to come down there in case they have to start evacuating houses around the area. Hopefully, they'll be able to contain the fire."

"I wonder if the killer…" I started to trail off as I thought about what evidence could have been in the house.

"Lenny, promise me that you'll stay here until I come back. We'll go look for the box after the fire danger is over." He said and kissed me on the forehead before rushing out.

"He didn't even wait for me to actually promise." I said to Aunt Kara.

"Brat, no. He didn't wait for you to respond because he trusts you."

"Aunt Kara, I have to go. I need to know, and if the fire does get out of control, we could lose the newspaper office. That box of letters could be there, and it might be the only clues we have." I fished her keys out of my purse. "Please, Aunt Kara, let me take your car."

"Fine, but I'm going with you." She said and stood up from her chair.

"Aunt Kara, no. You're already too close to this, and you need to stay clear of all of it until we've exonerated you for sure."

"Then you can't have my car."

"Fine."

We drove towards the newspaper office in silence. I could just see the smoke over the trees off in the distance where Lester's house burned. It made me a little queasy, and I hoped that Nathan would be okay.

"You did put a protection spell on him before he left, right?" Jezebel's voice scared me half out of my skin.

"Jezebel, what are you doing?" I screeched as I tried to turn the wheel and make the car go straight again.

"Lady, you didn't think I was going to let you two go solve this thing and steal all of the glory, did you?" Jez said and then stretched out on the back seat.

I pulled into the Tribune's parking area and killed the engine. Aunt Kara and I got out of the car quietly and left Jezebel sleeping in the back. She wanted to come in with us, but I wanted to keep her safe.

Aunt Kara and I got inside the office and I looked quickly through the two boxes of letters I found by Charle's desk. Neither of them were letters from Lester. There was another box of letters next to the empty desk, but it wasn't what I needed either.

I was about to give up when I remembered Charles bringing my laptop down from the attic. "Stay here. Make sure the door is locked. I'm going up to the attic to check. If it's not there, we'll go home." I told Kara.

Eleven

My heart fell into my stomach when I got up to the storage space above the offices. There were several boxes just inside the door, and I could feel down in my bones that what I was looking for was inside of one of them.

Lester's letters to Connie were in the third box I opened. I had to get them to Sherriff Brad. It occurred to me that the killer could have just stashed them here, and the murderer was framing Charles. However, that didn't change the fact that I had to get this evidence into the Sherriff's hands. As far as I knew, Aunt Kara had no access to the newspaper offices, and that meant that these letters further exonerated her.

My heart might have fallen into my stomach when I saw the boxes upstairs, but the scene when I got downstairs with the box made my blood run cold.

Aunt Kara was duck taped to my office chair, and standing behind her with a gun to her head was none other than Constance Piper. I was really going to have to get better at this.

"This is unexpected." I said as coolly as I could manage.

"You could have just left it alone. Your Aunt got out of the clinker, and ya'll should have just went

on with your lives. You had to meddle, though."
Connie said.

All of the emotion I'd seen in her earlier was gone.
I could now see that she was stone cold on the
inside.

"Why, Constance? Lester loved you." I tried to
swallow back the frog in my throat.

"He didn't want to get married again. It ticked me
off. I put two years of my time into turning that
moron into a proper husband, and then he had the
nerve to ask me why love wasn't enough." Connie
said and cackled like someone who was
completely unhinged.

"But, how did you get Aunt Kara's knife set?"

"That was too easy. Lester was changing
lightbulbs in the bed and breakfast's storage area,
and I noticed the door to Kara's personal store
room was open just a crack. I was bored, so I
popped in and looked around while Lester did his
work. He didn't even see me take the knives up
through the cellar door. Lester was always kind of
a dim wit. I wasn't even sure if I was going to kill
him until that day." Constance said and held the
gun closer to Kara's head.

"But what about David? Why did you kill him?" I asked. I had to keep her talking until I figured out what to do.

"He got the good columns when we worked at the paper. He always got to cover the good stories too. I hated him. I was the better writer. I could never figure out why he was so successful when I was more creative. So, I killed him too. I figured I might as well get everybody that annoys me out of the way."

"You're nuts." Aunt Kara said.

"And now you're annoying me too." Connie said as she cocked the gun.

"No, please don't. We can work this out." I begged.

"How are we supposed to work this out?" Constance laughed so hard that she snorted.

"Hey, Lady, I've got a way we can work this out." Jezebel's voice came from behind Constance and Aunt Kara.

Connie spun around and searched the room for the person speaking to her. Her eyes settled on the cat, and that's the moment that Jezebel spoke again.

"Hi, Lady. How's it going?" Jezebel taunted.

Constance was so shocked by the sight of my talking cat that she dropped the gun. I dove for it, but Connie tried to kick it across the room.

Aunt Kara managed to catch the gun with her foot, and I scrambled on my hands and knees to get to it before Constance could reclaim the weapon. She lunged for me, but Jezebel jumped up on her shoulders and started clawing her sweater set and biting at her hair.

Constance managed to get Jezebel off her shoulders, but I already had the gun. I raised it up and aimed it right at her chest. I'd watched enough cop shows and action movies to know it was better to aim at center mass than her head.

"Okay crazy lady, you're going to sit down and shut up." I said triumphantly.

Epilogue

In case you're wondering, Jezebel got in by climbing down the chimney. Sometimes curiosity kills the cat, and sometimes it saves your life.

Constance was ranting and raving when they arrested her about my talking cat, but considering she'd killed two men, took us hostage at gunpoint, and had probably started a fire, Sherriff Brad just figured she was nutzo.

The good news is that the firefighters got the blaze out before it spread to the surrounding forest. The bad news is that Nathan was less than pleased with me for going to the Tribune's office without him.

He forgave me right away. We took Kara and Jezebel home, and then he took me out for pie. If I'm going to get pie every time I upset him, I think he just might be the one.

Thank you for reading!

Made in the USA
Monee, IL
15 November 2023

46618844R00072